TO TYSHANA AND AJAHNI–SG

TO MY STRONG AND BEAUTIFUL MOM, CHRIS SNAGG THOMAS,
FOR ACCEPTING AND CELEBRATING MY WILD SELF (AND HAIR)–KT

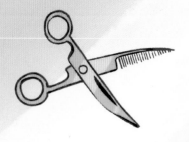

PENGUIN WORKSHOP
An imprint of Penguin Random House LLC, New York

First published in the United States of America by Penguin Workshop,
an imprint of Penguin Random House LLC, New York, 2022

Text copyright © 2022 by Shauntay Grant
Illustrations copyright © 2022 by Katelan Thomas

Visit us online at penguinrandomhouse.com.

Library of Congress Cataloging-in-Publication Data is available.

Manufactured in China

ISBN 9780593387085   10 9 8 7 6 5 4 3 2 1 HH

Design by Mary Claire Cruz

MY FADE IS FRESH

BY SHAUNTAY GRANT
ILLUSTRATED BY KITT THOMAS

Penguin Workshop

Yesterday at ten o'clock,
I walked into the barbershop.

My bushy, brownish, biggish hair
was growing almost everywhere.

"What to do?" the barber said.

"A PERM?"

"A PRESS?"

"A TRIM?"

"A CHOP?"

"Uh-uh," I said and shook my head.

"THE FRESHEST FADE UP ON THE BLOCK!"

"How 'bout a trim
that tucks it in?"

"A frizzy 'FRO that's neat and round."

"Or parted with a parting comb and **CORNROWS** braided to the ground."

"Just cut the tips and trim the sides and brush it into one big **PUFF**."

"Like this?"

"That's right."

"What is this goopy, gooey stuff!?"

"A bit of this, a LOT of that—you'll want it greasy-glossy groomed."

"How 'bout some SPIKES?"　　"Or TWISTS?"　　"Or LOCS?"

"MY WORD! IT'S ALMOST HALF PAST NOON!"

SPIKES?

"How 'bout an ocean cave with rocks and fish and giant waves?"

"You think that you
could write her name?"

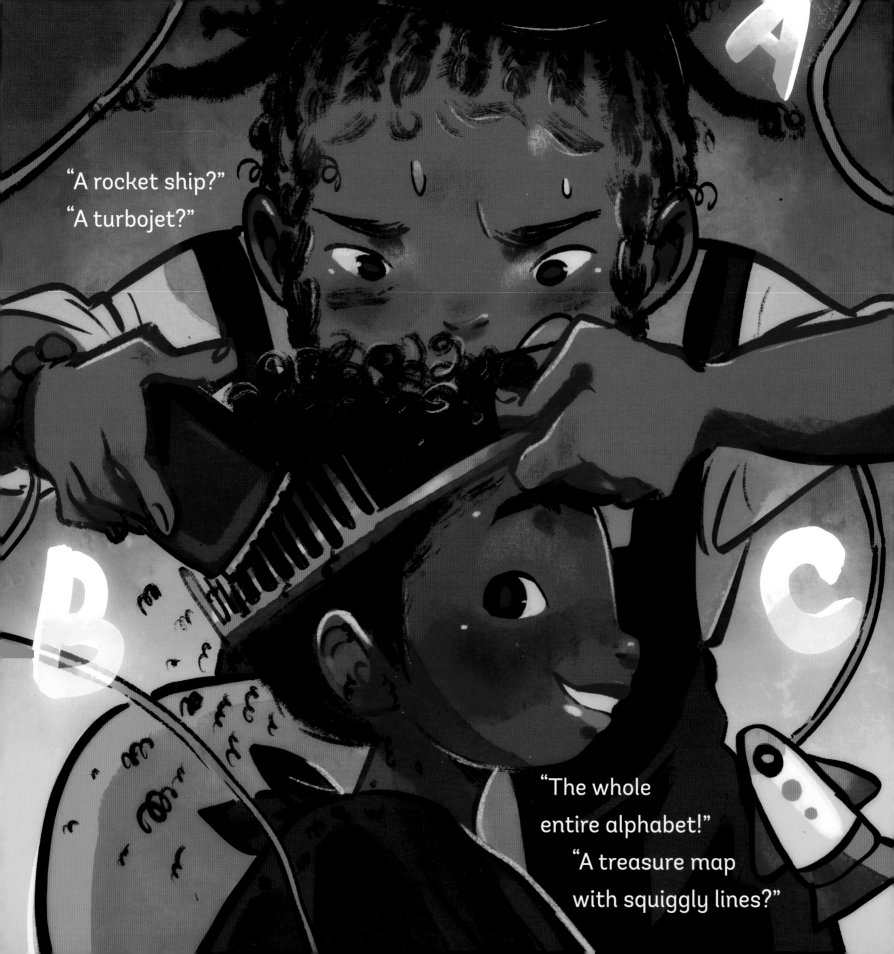

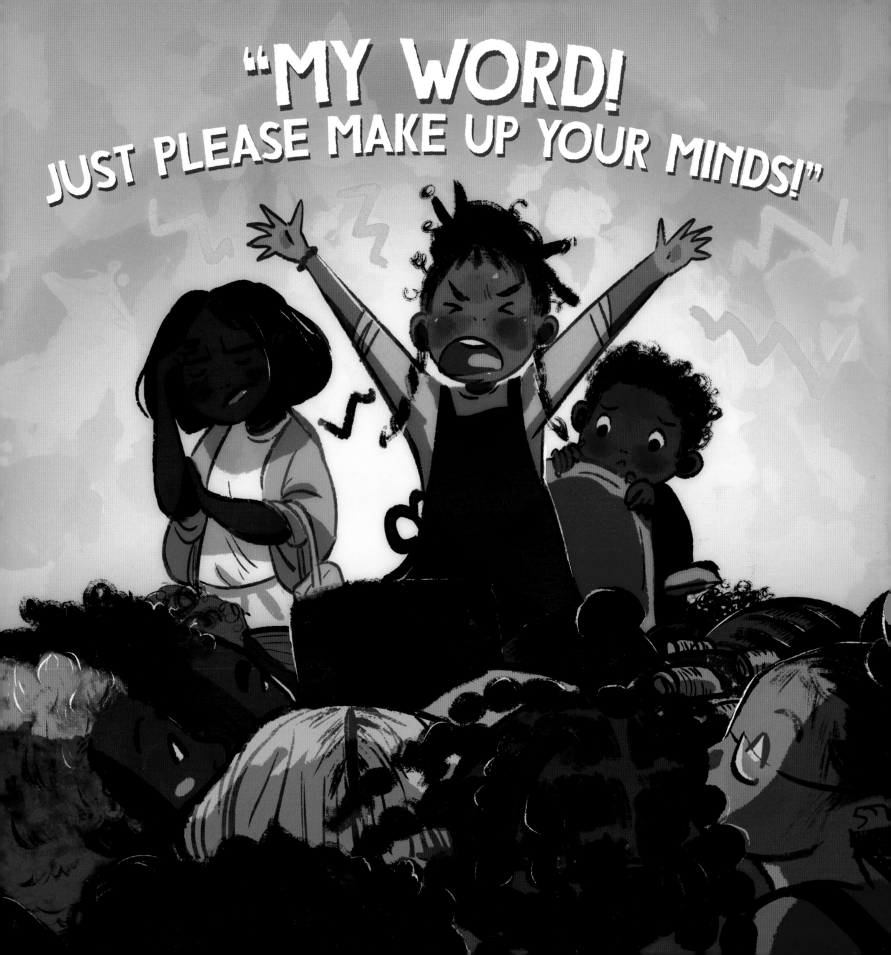

"Don't stress," I said.
"Just line me up."

So today 'round two o'clock, I walked right by the barbershop.

A clean-cut, classic curly crop.

THE FRESHEST FADE UP ON THE BLOCK.

7